Lots of love to Paul and Sue Davies – SM
For Cheryl, Louise, Petrona and Aniyah – CG

LITTLE TIGER PRESS LTD,
an imprint of the Little Tiger Group
1 Coda Studios, 189 Munster Road, London SW6 6AW
Imported into the EEA by Penguin Random House Ireland,
Morrison Chambers, 32 Nassau Street, Dublin D02 YH68
www.littletiger.co.uk

First published in Great Britain 2021

Illustrations by Carly Gledhill
Text and illustrations copyright © Little Tiger Press Ltd 2021

NOTHING SCARES SPIDER!

S MARENDAZ   CARLY GLEDHILL

LITTLE TIGER

LONDON

Spider was planning
a big adventure.
She was going to
be an explorer.

SPIDER'S
HOUSE

"I'm going to see the Whole Wide Garden," cheered Spider. And she went to say goodbye to her friends.

Caterpillar, Ladybird and Bumblebee
thought an adventure sounded scary.

"What about the Fearsome Fishies?
The Hungry Birdies? And the Hairy
B-b-beasties?" they asked.

Spider just laughed.
"Spiders aren't scared of
anything," she said.

"But who will protect US?"
her friends wailed.

"I'll leave a web so you can
call me back," said Spider.
"But only in emergencies."

~Yum, lunch!

Spider skipped to
the Tall Tall Trees.

She wasn't scared
of Hungry Birdies.

"Ha!" Spider laughed.

"What is it?
What is it?" said Spider.

It was Ladybird.
   "Oh Spider!" she flapped.
"Someone's in my flower!"

"That's just Bumblebee!" said Spider.
"Phew!" said Ladybird. "Thanks!"
"This web is only for emergencies!" said
Spider. "I'm very busy with my adventure!"

And she set off
once more.

Spider skipped to the Big Blue Pond.
She wasn't scared of Fearsome Fishies.

"Ha ha!" laughed Spider.
But just then . . .

— Ooh, tasty!

TWANG!

An emergency!

Spider rushed
home at once.

"What is it? What is it?" cried Spider.
"Oh Spider," gulped Caterpillar. "There's something huge and scary behind me!"
"That's just your shadow!" said Spider.

"So it is," said Caterpillar. "Silly me!"
"Caterpillar! I told you – this web is
only for emergencies!" said Spider.
"You're interrupting my adventure."
And off she went.

Spider skipped to the Lush Long Grass.
She wasn't scared of Hairy Beasties. Not one bit.
"Ha ha ha!" laughed Spider.

But just then . . .

TWANG!

It had to be an emergency this time!
Right?

"What is it now?" she asked Bumblebee.
"Ummm . . . I heard a scary
buzzing noise!" said Bumblebee.
"That's you," said Spider. She
was starting to feel very cross.

"Phew!" said Bumblebee.
"That was close!"

Buzz
Buzz

"It wasn't close because there's nothing scary in the flowerbed now please leave the web alone!" Spider shouted, and she stomped off to continue her adventure in peace.

Spider travelled further and further away.

But just then . . .

YAN

Spider was tugged all the way back home
and straight into – an emergency!
"The Frightening Frog is going to eat us!"
cried her friends.

HELP!

But Spider wasn't scared.

"Oi YOU!"

she shouted.

The frog turned on Spider.
His yellow eyes gleamed . . .

EEK!

Now the Frightening Frog
was going to eat her.

And Spider was scared.
Very scared!

"Quick, Spider!" called Caterpillar. "We can stop him if we work together."
So Spider span a web . . . and Ladybird and Bumblebee dropped it on the frog's head.

"We'll let you out if you buzz off!" they all told him.

And he did!

"Thank you for saving us," said
Spider's friends. "We tried
to be brave, like you."

"You saved me!" said Spider. "I suppose that even spiders are scared sometimes. On my next adventure you're all coming with me. In case of emergencies!"

Have your own big adventure with these Little Tiger books.

PATRICIA HEGARTY · ALEX WILLMORE

SUPERHERO BABY!

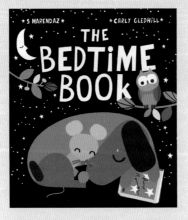

S MARENDAZ · CARLY GLEDHILL

THE BEDTIME BOOK

IMPOSSIBLE!

Tracey Corderoy · Tony Neal

Oh NO, BEAR!

JOANNE PARTIS

Timothy Knapman · Steve James

THUNDER DOWN UNDER

MEET THE **GRUMBLIES**

JOHN KELLY · CARMEN SALDANA

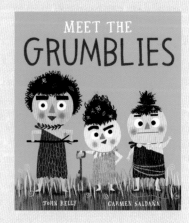

LITTLE TIGER

For information regarding any of the above titles or for our catalogue, please contact us: Little Tiger Press Ltd, 1 Coda Studios, 189 Munster Road, London SW6 6AW • Tel: 020 7385 6333
E-mail: contact@littletiger.co.uk • www.littletiger.co.uk